TRACTOR MAC
AUTUMN IS HERE

Written and illustrated by

BILLY STEERS

FARRAR STRAUS GIROUX · NEW YORK

EVENINGS WERE GETTING COOLER at Stony Meadow Farm. The colors on the farm changed almost overnight from greens and blues to a riot of golds, scarlets, and rusts.

"This is my favorite time of year," said Tractor Mac.

Sibley agreed. "I love the new smells of earth and hay."

"I brought a fresh load of pumpkins to the farm stand this morning. Fall into autumn!" said Sibley with a chuckle.

"I can't wait to try out my new mounted corn picker this year. It will be a nice change from my old tow-behind harvester," said Tractor Mac.

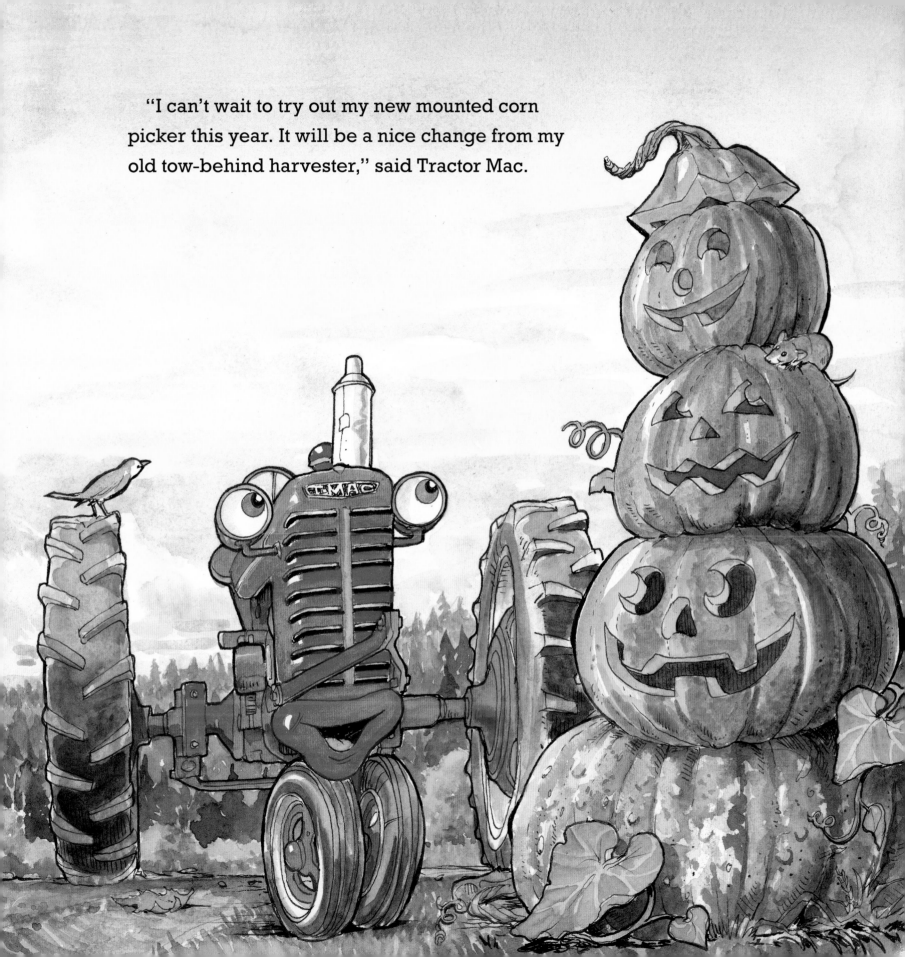

Not everybody was happy with the changes that fall brings.

"I'm very worried about my little calf, Fergus," mooed Fergie the cow to Tractor Mac. "He was just born last spring, so this is his first autumn."

"Things change so fast here this time of year, and Fergus does not like change," added Margot.

"That baby bovine is doomed, I tell you! A calf that doesn't like autumn? I never!" declared Goat Walter sagely.

"Oh, phoo, Walter. Fergie is worried enough without you," said Margot.

"Change is good!" clucked Carla the chicken. "Chicks hatch from eggs, tadpoles become frogs, caterpillars will be butterflies."

But Fergus did not understand why things had to change. He had a routine that he followed every day. First, Fergus frolicked in the tall grass with his friend Noah, making tunnels and paths. Next, he and Noah played a rousing game of hide-and-seek among the corn rows.

Then, Fergus would nap in the shade of
the big green oak tree before supper.

But one day, when Fergus arrived at the field where he and Noah played, the grasses and wildflowers were gone!

"Too barren!" said Fergus.

"Oh well. There's always the cornfield to play in," said Noah.

But the cornfield was also gone! Nothing but stubs of stalks remained.

"Too stubbly!" cried Fergus.

"We could play a different game," said Noah, but when he turned around, Fergus was gone. Fergus almost ran into Tractor Mac wearing his corn picker, he was so upset.

"Too scary!" bawled Fergus.

Fergus ran to his favorite big oak tree, but its leaves were now amber and brown. He slipped on a pile of acorns that were where he would normally lay in the shade.

"Too much!" wailed Fergus. He needed to find someplace that always remained the same.

"Change your pace, young calf! You almost bowled me over!" shouted Goat Walter.

Noah could not find his friend anywhere. He asked Fergie and his aunt Margot. He asked Sibley the horse. He asked Sam the ram.

"That crazy mini-bull ran that way," said Walter, who had been the last one to see Fergus.

"I have a hunch about where he might be," said Tractor Mac. "Fergus would want to find a place that doesn't change much."

The root cellar was a calm, snug place. The
temperature always stayed the same. The lighting
and the smells remained constant. It was dry, cool,
and quiet, and Fergus hoped it would never change.

"Come out so we can talk, Fergus," said Tractor Mac gently.

"We need to show you some things," said Sibley.

"It's okay to come outside, Fergus," urged Noah.

Tentatively, Fergus poked his head out of the root cellar.

Tractor Mac took Fergus over to the silo. "I use the corn picker to bring in the corn. The stalks get put into the silo and the ears of corn go into the cribs to feed all the animals through the year," explained Tractor Mac.

"I liked the cornstalks better when they stood in rows," moaned Fergus.

"The fields are cut for hay to feed us
and for straw for our bedding," said Sibley.

"The fields get to rest through the winter;
then they'll grow new crops in the spring,"
added Sam the ram.

"I think the hay was better when it grew
as grass and flowers in the field,"
complained Fergus.

"I know you're unhappy about the leaves falling off the trees, but the trees aren't dead, they're just getting ready to sleep through the winter," said Sharon the sheep.

"The leaves help the soil, and the falling nuts and seeds will feed animals. Some will grow into new trees," said Tractor Mac.

Fergus thought about the leaves spiraling off the trees and the acorns on the ground as his friends walked him home. Fergie and Margot were very happy to see him.

As the weeks went on, Fergus watched the changes around him. "I was so sad when the blossoms fell off the trees in the spring. But look at all the apples in their place now!" Fergus said to Noah.

"Jumping in leaf piles is a fun game!" cheered Noah.

"Mine is a leaf fort!" said Fergus.

"Who knew you could build an igloo out of hay bales?" said Noah.

"And make a hay-bale wall to protect it!" Fergus chimed in.

Sometimes Fergus still felt sad about autumn, like when his bird friends migrated away. But new friends arrived from the north to overwinter at the farm.

"I'm glad they fill the feeders here,"
said a little gray-and-white bird.

As fall progressed, children came to visit Fergus and the other animals at Stony Meadow Farm on weekends and school breaks. Then, Fergus got to see a lot of his friends at the Pumpkin Picking Festival.

Fergus watched the signs of the changing season and marveled at the changing colors.

"Thank you, Tractor Mac, for showing me that change can be good," said Fergus.

"I like the change in you, Fergus," said Tractor Mac. "Happy autumn!"

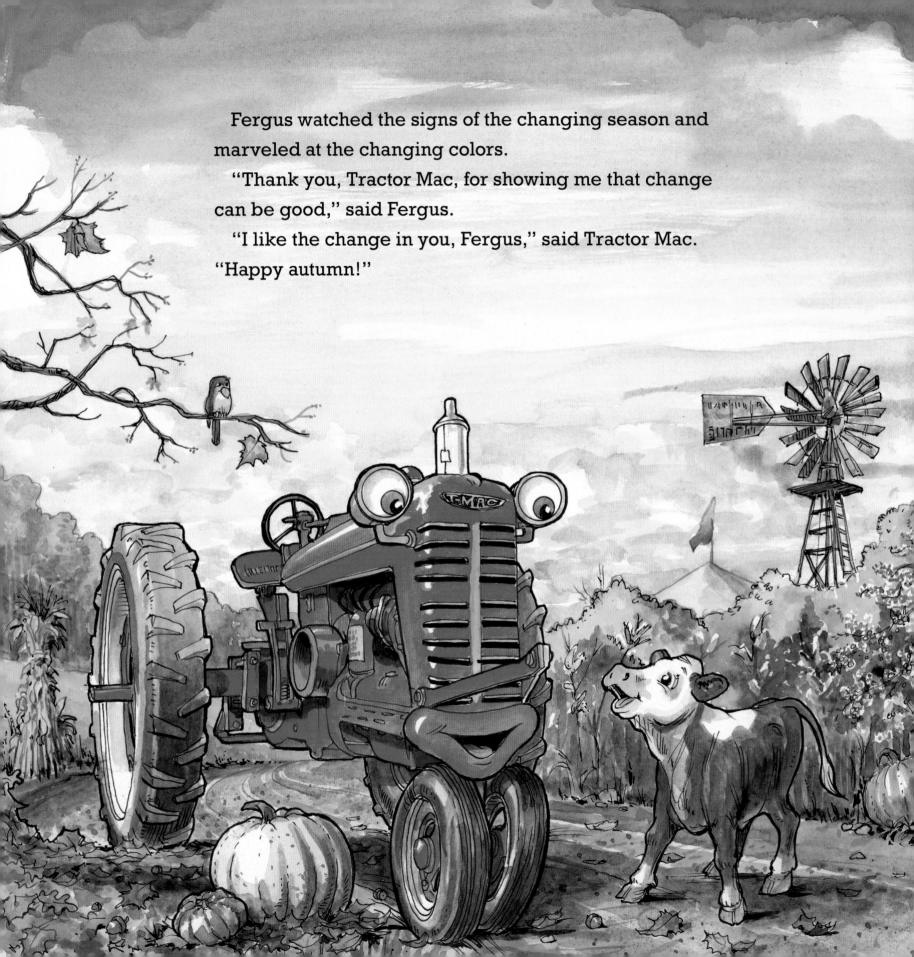

To Trip, Willy, and Nate, who have changed from
fantastic little boys into fine young men

Farrar Straus Giroux Books for Young Readers
An imprint of Macmillan Publishing Group, LLC
120 Broadway, New York, NY 10271

Copyright © 2019 by Billy Steers
All rights reserved
Color separations by Bright Arts (H.K.) Ltd.
Printed in China by Toppan Leefung Printing Ltd.,
Dongguan City, Guangdong Province
First edition, 2019

1   3   5   7   9   10   8   6   4   2

mackids.com

Library of Congress Cataloging-in-Publication Data

Names: Steers, Billy, author, illustrator.
Title: Tractor Mac autumn is here / written and illustrated by Billy Steers.
Other titles: Autumn is here
Description: First edition. | New York : Farrar Straus Giroux, 2019. |
   Series: Tractor Mac | Summary: At Stony Meadow Farm, Fergus the calf does
   not like change and misses summer's flowers and shade trees until Tractor
   Mac helps him appreciate the changes autumn brings, such as colorful
   leaves, pumpkin festivals, and apples.
Identifiers: LCCN 2018035840 | ISBN 9780374309206 (hardcover)
Subjects: | CYAC: Autumn—Fiction. | Seasons—Fiction. | Farm life—Fiction.
   | Change—Fiction. | Cows—Fiction. | Domestic animals—Fiction. |
   Tractors—Fiction.
Classification: LCC PZ7.S81536 Tqd 2019 | DDC [E]—dc23
LC record available at https://lccn.loc.gov/2018035840

Our books may be purchased in bulk for promotional, educational, or business use.
Please contact your local bookseller or the Macmillan Corporate and Premium Sales Department
at (800) 221-7945 ext. 5442 or by email at MacmillanSpecialMarkets@macmillan.com.

ABOUT THE AUTHOR

Billy Steers is an author, illustrator, and commercial pilot. In addition to the Tractor Mac series, he has worked on forty other children's books. Mr. Steers raised horses and sheep on the farm where he grew up in Connecticut. Married with three sons, he still lives in Connecticut. Learn more about the Tractor Mac books at tractormac.com.

ALSO BY BILLY STEERS